VIKING KESTREL
Viking Penguin Inc., 40 West 23rd Street
New York, New York 10010, U.S.A.
Penguin Books Canada Limited, 2801 John Street
Markham, Ontario, Canada L3R 1B4

First published in 1989 by Viking Penguin Inc.
Published simultaneously in Canada
Set in Sabon.
Printed and bound in Italy
Created and Produced by Sadie Fields Productions Ltd,
8, Pembridge Studios, 27A Pembridge Villas, London W11 3EP

1   2   3   4   5   93   92   91   90   89

I Like To Help

Karen Erickson and Maureen Roffey

Viking Kestrel

Help? I'm not good at helping.
I want to play. I want to do
what I want to do.

But Mom says in a family
each person has to help out.
She says I'm part of a team.

Well, I'll try. I'll help a little.

Wow. I made my bed
and it didn't take long.

Hey, I set the table
and everything looks great!

See, I played with my baby brother
and he's smiling!

Look, I helped my family.

Helping makes me feel good.

Helping makes me feel grown-up.

You never know how helping feels
until you try it.

Now I know I can help.

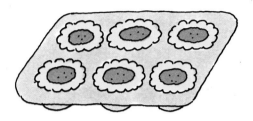

I can do it.
I did it.